Core Signs Glossary

We've split our book into two parts; the **core** signs that we suggest that you sign throughout the book and the **supplementary** signs (which you will find at the back of the book) that you may like to use with older children, or when you are more familiar with the core signs.

You'll find the sign graphics are repeated, in the order in which they are used, on the relevant pages to give you a handy visual reminder along the way.

Little ones will love to join in with finding the correct sign for you and delight in showing you their ability to sign for themselves.

* Signs vary - lots! You can find the alternative sign for Frog in the Supplementary Signs Glossary.

Bee
O' hand moves forward and left with smooth quick twisting movements from the wrist.

Butterfly
Hands are crossed with palms facing towards body. Interlock thumbs and make flapping movements with fingers held together.

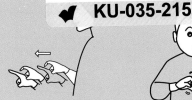

Caterpillar
Index finger moves forward, flexing repeatedly.

Crawly (insect)
Fingers of palm down hand wiggle as hand moves forward.

Fly
'O' hand moves forward and left with jerky quick twisting movements from the wrist.

Frog*
Full 'C' hand makes short forward and backward movement near throat.

Garden
Right flat hand twists from the wrist in repeated scooping movements.

Grasshopper
Right 'V' hand sits bent on left palm down flat hand. Right hand flexes forward and up, then back down again.

Ladybird
Index finger strokes along cheekbone; palm down hand then moves down and wiggles forwards.

Slug
Index fingers of both hands move to head and bend forwards.

Smile
Index fingers at sides of mouth move in upward arcs in shape of wide smile.

Snail
Right 'V' hand pushes forward and up from under left bent hand.

Special
Palm 'O' hands make two short movements forward. One hand can be used.

Spider
Fingers of palm down right clawed hand wriggle and the hand moves up and down.

Worm
Palm left right index finger flexes repeatedly as hand moves forward.

At the bottom of my garden
I have a special place;

Garden

Special

'Again, again!' must be the enduring memory of any person who has had the privilege to read aloud to young children. Well loved stories that are requested over and again until such time that the little one concerned can recite the tale they love, so well, by heart.

And so starts our earliest journey into literacy and language – cherished memories of choosing a story with care, being lifted to a special lap for snuggles and undivided attention as a new adventure unfolds.

Over many years of observation and research we've come to know that laughter, smiles and eye contact form the basis of the very best part of cognitive development, providing a platform for peak learning experiences. One of the simplest tools to support this platform is that of baby signing – or gesture communication – in conjunction with speech. It is, without doubt, the bridge between communication and language.

Despite its name, baby signing is very definitely not just for babies but provides support for toddlers with emerging speech and adds layers of learning for older children. Signing is quite literally 'language in motion' and, as children learn best by doing, it helps children not only to learn more ably but to retain that information and recall it more easily.

Children of all ages and abilities love stories. Using books with signing is the perfect vehicle for enhanced interactions - which in turn support good language and communication skills.

At the Bottom of my Garden is our second 'Rhyme and Sign Adventure; we've been sure to include all of those things you loved so much when reading **Our Farmyard Friends.** A rhyming and repetitive story line (enabling little ones to join in easily), beautiful illustrations (we invite you to spot the surprise additions!) and the enjoyment you will get from signing will mean that it too becomes a much loved tale in your library - returned to time and again.

From us, to you, with love.

Sue   *Shelley*

Always say the word as you sign it
Sign in your little one's line of vision
Repeat signs and words – lots!

"This is a lovely story in its own right but it's actually much more than that.

There's lots of rhyme and repetition which are important for supporting language learning and developing vocabulary - plus the addition of signs which can help enhance early literacy and learning.

You don't need any signing experience to be able to use this book straight away. It's an accessible and enjoyable tale for all ages from babies to grandparents.

They'll all love to join in!"

Libby Hill
Consultant Speech and Language Therapist
Small Talk Speech and Language Therapy

Getting the most out of your 'Rhyme and Sign' Adventure

You don't need to sign every word

When signing to songs with young children pick a sign or two per sentence. They love to join in and feel capable – too many signs in a sentence will feel overwhelming as their little hands will struggle to join in.

Slow it down

Being mindful of little fingers, slow down. It might feel strange at first to speak more slowly but the children will be able to engage more fully. As you sign, look to see any attempt to join in. Wait for a moment or two and then move on to the next part. This allows everyone to join in and will reduce frustration about missing the next sign or part of the story whilst concentrating on something prior.

Be dramatic and engaging

Many signs are accompanied by over-exaggerated facial expressions. Its good to practise this with little people as they really get involved with stories with their whole bodies. It will help with identification of feelings - and for those children who find emotions of others difficult to define, it can add a new understanding.

Enable everyone to join in

Signing stories in English word order means that there are more frequent visual cues for young children; they can anticipate what is happening and are able to join in more easily.

Frequent repetition

You'll have found that young children like to hear their favourite stories over and over again. When using signing, stories are absorbed more readily and the signs will quickly become a natural part of their communication.

Attention and Observation

We've added some surprise additions throughout the book and these invite children of all ages to go on a bug hunt! You'll have huge fun together whilst your little one develops their attention and observation abilities - critical pre-reading and literacy skills.

Facilitate more effective learning

Children are kinaesthetic learners which means that they learn more ably when they are involved with what they are doing. Signing is literally 'language in motion' and using signs with favourite stories helps to:

✓ promote better communication ✓ increase confidence
✓ builds a larger word bank ✓ improve literacy skills
✓ facilitate more effective learning

Helpful Tips for Hand Shapes

Bunched Hand
The finger ends and thumb are all bunched together

Bent Hand
The fingers are together and straight, then bent at the palm knuck[l]

Closed Hand
The hand is closed with thumb against index finger

Full C Hand
The thumb is curv[ed] and the fingers ar[e] together, curved i[n] C shape

Flat Hand
Hand is held flat with all fingers straight and together

O Hand
The tip of the ind[ex] finger touches the tip of the thumb t[o] form an 'O' shape

Clawed Hand
The fingers are extended and bent, spread apart

V Hand
The index and middle fingers are extended and spread apart.

Where all the little crawly things
have a smile upon their face...

Crawly
(insect)

Smile

Leaf

Caterpillar

Sun

Butterfly

Hiding, underneath this leaf,
all shiny, fresh and green...
Meet my friend, Caterpillar,
the fluffiest one I've seen!

Who's inside this snuggly home
and dreams of flying in the sun?

Look! Look! It's Butterfly
- flying round for fun.

At the bottom of my garden
I have a special place;

Garden

Special

Crawly
(insect)

Where all the little crawly things have a smile upon their face...

Smile   Caterpillar   Butterfly

Come and look underneath this rock;
You'll see it's cool and wet.
        Here we'll find Mister Worm,
            all wriggly and pink, I bet!

A trail that shines? It must be Slug!
He moves s l o w l y along the ground..
He's looking for somewhere safe to hide
and doesn't make a sound

Wet

Worm

Shiny

Slug

At the bottom of my garden
I have a special place;

Garden

Special

Crawly (insect)

Smile

Where all the little crawly things
have a smile upon their face...

Caterpillar

Butterfly

Worm

Slug

'Chirp Chirp'
says quick green Grasshopper
as he hops on by.
Can you jump as high as him?
I can! Almost to the sky.

Here's another of my friends -
she likes the compost pile.
Its Fly and her family,
they play here for a while.

Grasshopper

Jump

Rubbish

Fly

At the bottom of my garden
I have a special place;

Garden   Special   Crawly
(insect)   Smile   Caterpillar

Where all the little crawly things have a smile upon their face...

Butterfly

Worm

Slug

Grasshopper

Fly

Bee

Flower

Red

Ladybird

In my garden is a hive;
the home of Bumble Bee!
Watch him dance and wiggle
between the flowers and trees.

I'm looking for my
bright red friend.
Have you seen her yet?
Ladybird has a spotty coat
and doesn't like the wet.

At the bottom of my garden
I have a special place;

Garden   Special   Crawly (insect)   Smile   Caterpillar   Butterfly

Where all the little crawly things
have a smile upon their face...

Snail

Slow

Frog

Jump

Here is Snail with his curly shell and eyes on little stalks.

He glides along so s l o w l y, he hardly moves at all!

Oh! Frog!
You made me jump, landing next to me!

I love to hear you croaking
when you're catching
bugs for tea.

At the bottom of my garden
I have a special place;

How many signs can you remember?

Where all the little crawly things have a smile upon their face...

The bottom of my garden
is a special place for fun.
You've met almost all my friends here...

Garden Fun Friends

...all except for one!

Spider

Supplementary Signs Glossary

This book has been designed to grow with your little one and, as they become adept with basic signs, they will soon want to know more and more! If you have started to read this story with toddlers or older children, don't be surprised if they pick up signing very quickly indeed, sometimes immediately.

Include these signs once you feel comfortable with the core signs – or if your child is older and wants to learn more – but please don't feel overwhelmed.

Frog
Full 'C' hand makes short forward and backward movement near throat.

Frog
Fingers of right 'V' hand flex in hopping movements up left arm.

Flower
'O' hand moves from side to side under the nose.

Friends
Hands clasp together and shale forward / down several times.

Fun
'C' hands held under the chin, one above the other, jiggle in and out past each other as shoulders shake.

Jump
Right 'V' hand (legs classifier) jumps up flexing on left palm.

Leaf
Index fingers and thumbs move apart and close in outline shape of a leaf.

Red
Index finger flexes as it makes repeated small brushing movements near the lips.

Rubbish
Left fist is held as if lifting a lid as right full 'O' hand moves down sharply as it opens.

Shiny
Palm facing upwards hands move upwards, twisting quickly from the wrists.

Slow
Right palm down hand brushes from left wrist up the forearm.

Sun
Full 'O' hand moves down and in as the singers spring open at head height.

Wet
Fingers of bent hand open and close onto thumb several times. Two hands can be used.